FAIRY TALES

BY

HANS

CHRISTIAN

ANDERSEN

With Illustrations by Harrison Weir,
V. Pedersen, M. L. Stone, A. W. Bayes,
And Others

A Facsimile of the 1884 Edition

AVENEL BOOKS
NEW YORK

ISBN: 0-517-164825
Copyright © MCMLXXV by Crown Publishers, Inc.
Library of Congress Catalog Card Number: 75-695
This edition is published by Avenel Books
a division of Barre Publishing, Inc.
h
Manufactured in the United States of America

CONTENTS

HANS CHRISTIAN ANDERSEN.

Life of Andersen.

HANS CHRISTIAN ANDERSEN was the only child of poor parents. He was born at Odense, on the island of Funen, on the 2d of April, 1805. The town of Odense has been immortalized by Andersen in one of his tales, "The Bell-Deep," which is no doubt founded on a legend he had been acquainted with from his childhood.

Hans Andersen's father was a shoemaker, who, it is said, had not the means of giving him much education, but he sent him to the grammar school in the town, and the boy's natural abilities and love of reading made him take advantage of the instruction he there received. Not, however, for long; his father's death, in 1814, left his mother a sorrowing widow, in poor circumstances, with an orphan boy of nine years. It therefore became necessary for him to leave school, and try to help his mother in earning a home for them both. An opportunity for him to work at a factory in the town was offered to his mother, and eagerly accepted by her, and for some years he worked as a factory boy.

There was something, however, so different in the coarse and illiterate workmen at the factory, to the refined and tender-hearted child, that his patient sufferings of their taunts and torments must have been terrible to bear. At last he complained to his mother, and she removed him. An

opening for the youth, now in his four-
teenth year, to become a tailor presented
itself; but the boy of intellectual tastes
implored his mother, even with tears, to
allow him to choose his own career in
life. His mother at last consented, and
with a small sum of money in his pocket,
he left his home to travel to Copenhagen
alone.

Who can tell how much of a mother's
love and pride in her son gave her the
courage to part with him, and to utter a
farewell which cost her so much? No doubt
she already looked forward to a glorious
future for her imaginative child, who most
probably inherited from her the refined
and poetic fancy which in after years made
him so famous.

Her fancies, indeed, had a tinge of the
superstition still holding sway in the land
of the Norsemen; and, strange to say, she
looked forward to a time when her son
should revisit his native town, and Odense
would be illuminated in his honor. This
really happened many years afterwards,
when the great poet and author, covered

with glory and fame, entered the town of his birth.

And now the boy of fourteen was launched on the ocean of life to seek for that renown which only became his after years of disappointment and trial. How little he was appreciated in the great city was well known. From early childhood his keen susceptibility to the emotions of joy or sorrow made them sometimes overpowering. At nine years of age he had laughed at a comedy, or wept at a tragedy performed on the stage by marionettes! and in after years, the real, living actors would move him with equal power.

On his arrival at Copenhagen, he met with a friend in one of the professors at the University, and as the boy was fond of music, he proposed that Andersen should learn to sing on the stage. But this effort failed, for the boy's voice, though harmonious, was thin and weak, and could not be heard even at a moderate distance.

After some years of struggling to earn a living, even while writing down the curi-

ous thoughts with which his imagination
teemed, he determined to visit Germany; but
his friend had obtained for him instruction

THE FACTORY.

in Latin and German, which enabled him
to remain and to bring out in 1829 his first
work, a play entitled "The Life of a Nico-

laton," which was very successful ; and in the next year he published his first story, and soon after another—" Shadow Pictures."

In 1832 he carried out his intention and visited Germany, and here his books at once obtained notice, which gave him courage to continue the work he so loved, with renewed zeal. During the years from 1832 to 1848 Andersen wrote his far-famed works, a " Picture Book without Pictures ;" "The Improvisatore ;" " He was only an Actor ;" " The Story of the Year," and several others.

But the works that made him famous were his " Fairy Tales," the first of which appeared in 1838, while others so quickly followed that they obtained for Hans Andersen the name of " The Children's Friend."

In the early part of Andersen's career, he had been greatly pained, but not daunted, by the severe and even mocking criticisms which his writings received, in Copenhagen especially.

The first to notice them were the editors

of comic periodicals, and in these they were criticised and made a mock of, often with a want of delicacy most painful to the sensitive author. By others his style was pronounced to be intricate, confused, and crude. At the same time, it was acknowledged that the writer possessed great power of language, and a remarkable richness of thought and imagination, rendering the word-pictures his fancy drew too attractive to be passed over unread.

One of Andersen's oldest friends was Count Conrad of Rantzsan-Breitenburgh. This gentleman, who had been Prime Minister in the Duchy of Schleswig-Holstein, had given Andersen his first step as an author, which the narrow limits of his own poor dwelling rendered almost impossible. The Count had, however, heard of him, sought him out, and recognized at once that the humble-minded young writer was destined to become a popular poet and author.

This was the turning point in Andersen's career; the unkind criticisms referred to had so disheartened him that he was

tempted to despair of success. The Count's
opinion gave him fresh courage and energy
for renewed efforts, which, as we now
know, brought him glory and fame.

When the Count left Copenhagen he did
not forget Andersen, but made him promise that at the first opportunity he would
come and visit him at Castle Breitenburgh.
The opportunity presented itself after some
years, and Andersen used to say that the
weeks and months of his stay at Castle
Breitenburgh, belonged to the most beautiful period of his life, and truly he might
say this; for Count Conrad, the owner
of the castle, was in the highest degree a
man calculated to arouse and console the
tender-hearted, poetic, and often sad spirit
of his guest.

Andersen was one of those clever men
who are totally devoid of vanity, and he
would often express in a straightforward
and touching manner his modest opinion
of his own talents, and yet at the same time
acknowledge how greatly he longed for
and needed encouragement. And all this
time within his soul, his thoughts were

pressing full on his creative fancy which he longed to send forth to the world, yet dreaded with pain these adverse criticisms. Not even in his old age, when he had been recognized by the whole civilized world as a poet and author, could Andersen harden himself to treat with indifference the unjust criticism of the most insignificant critic.

Count Conrad died in the year 1844, while Andersen was in Germany, and the loss of such a friend was to the poet very great. And although he was now a popular author, and often invited by the Danish and German nobility to visit them at their castles, the memory of his first kind friend, the owner of Breitenburgh Castle, held the foremost place in his heart.

He was popular in Denmark now, although his name as a story-writer was first recognized by the common people, who quickly appreciated and understood the vein of simplicity which runs through every page of Hans Andersen's tales. The characters in these stories, whether of men or animals, whether animate or inanimate, became living, breathing creatures when he read his stories aloud, for in spite of his humble birth, his pronunciation of his native language was pure, correct and noble. While listening, it seemed not impossible that the objects described might be beings possessing souls, and the power of becoming sad or joyous, sublime or ridiculous as the author represented.

In the year 1845, King Christian VIII., of Denmark, placed a very pleasant shooting box, situated in the thickest covert of the magnificent park of Fredericksburg, at the disposal of Hans Andersen, who had been a widower for many years. This unused building was now named "Pheasant Court;" it had a large garden and was to be used by the poet as his own for life.

It was about this time that Andersen made a tour of the different countries of Europe, and those who knew him personally speak with delight of having met him at dinner parties, and of the glowing descriptions he would give of the places he had visited, and the persons he had met during his travels. Scottish scenery charmed him, and he would speak of Sir

Walter Scott and Robert Burns, to whom
he was introduced, in the most glowing
terms.

BREITENBURGH CASTLE.

Among his friends nearer home were the two renowned Swedish ladies, "Frederika Bremer, and Jenny Lind," both of whom had a touching sisterly affection for the poet.

His love of flowers was a poet's love of the beautiful, and even from the first appearance of that decay of nature which was to remove him at last from earth, he would have fresh flowers in his room daily, often remarking on their beauty and fragrance.

In 1872, Andersen had suffered from a severe illness while visiting at Rolighed, the country residence of a merchant named Melchior. Finding himself, as he thought, better, he returned home, but was still obliged to keep in his room.

In the spring of 1873 he traveled to Switzerland, and there went through a course of goat's milk, among the mountains at Glion, on the lake of Geneva. He there became so much better and stronger that he was able to take long drives, and returned to his home full of hope that his health was quite restored. But this hope soon faded, and in the spring of 1875 it became evident that his days were numbered. But he was not forsaken by his friends. Frau Melchior watched over him with tender care, and as the summer passed and he became weaker, she had him removed to their country house, Rolighed.

The king came to visit him many times, and the crown prince much oftener, and he was also visited frequently by men and women of high position. Not only were his last days brightened by these attentions, but from his own hopeful and poetical character.

Days passed, and as he grew weaker he was greatly comforted by the tender care that surrounded him, and while talking with his visitors he would often cut out and paste together a little figure in which the poetic art would show itself, even as in his fairy tales the charm of the characters introduced would represent his own poetic imagination.

Hans Christian Andersen died August 4th, 1875, at the age of 70. He had on that day been sleeping peacefully for some hours and at about eleven o'clock at night **Frau**

Melchior left the bedside for a moment,
and when she returned, after scarcely two
minutes absence, he was dead.

ANDERSEN'S MONUMENT.

The Last Dream

<small>OF THE</small>

Old Oak.

HIGH up on the steep shore, and not far from the open sea, stood a very old oak tree. It was just three hundred and sixty-five years old, but that was to the tree as the same number of days might be to us. We wake by day and sleep by night. It is different with the tree; it is obliged to keep awake through three seasons of the year, and does not get any sleep till winter comes. Winter is its time for rest—its night after the long day of spring, summer, and autumn. On many a warm summer, the flies, that exist only for a day, had fluttered about the old oak, enjoyed life and felt happy; and if, for a moment, one of the tiny creatures rested on one of his large, fresh leaves, the tree would always say, " Poor little creature! your whole life consists only of a single day. How very short. It must be quite melancholy."

" What do you mean ?" the little creature would reply. " Everything around me is so wonderfully bright and beautiful, that it makes me joyous."

"But only for one day, and then it is all over."

" Over," repeated the fly; "what is the meaning of that ? Are you all over, too ?"

" No; I shall very likely live for thousands of your days."

"Then I don't understand you. You may have thousands of my days, but I

have thousands of moments in which I can
be merry and happy. We have the same
time to live, only we reckon differently."
And the little creature danced and floated
in the air and was very happy. When the
sun sank low, it felt tired. Its wings could
sustain it no longer, and gently and slowly

it glided down upon the soft, waving
blades of grass, nodded its little head as
well as it could nod, and slept peacefully
and sweetly. The fly was dead.

"Poor little fly!" said the oak; "what a
terribly short life!" And so, on every
summer day the dance was repeated, the
same questions asked, and the same

answers given.   The same thing was repeated through many generations of flies.

The oak remained awake through the
morning of spring, the noon of summer,
and the evening of autumn; its time of
rest drew nigh—winter was coming, and
at last it fell asleep.

It was just about Christmas time that
the tree dreamed a dream.   All that had
happened during every year of his life
seemed to pass before him, as in a festive
procession.   Then it seemed as if new life
was thrilling through every fibre of root
and stem and leaf.   The tree felt itself
stretching and spreading out, while through
the root ran the warm vigor of life.   As
he grew higher and still higher, with in-
creased strength, his self-satisfaction in-
creased, and with it arose a joyous longing
to grow higher and higher, to reach even
to the warm, bright sun itself.   Already
had his topmost branches pierced the
clouds, which floated beneath them like
large white swans.   The stars became
visible in broad daylight, large and spark-
ling, like clear and gentle eyes.   These

were wonderful and happy moments for
the old tree, full of peace and joy; and
yet, amidst all this happiness, the tree felt
a yearning, longing desire that all the
other trees, bushes, herbs and flowers beneath him, might be able also to rise
higher, as he had done, and to see all this
splendor, and experience the same happiness. At length his longing was satisfied.
Up through the clouds came the green
summits of the forest trees, and beneath
him, the oak saw them rising, and growing
higher and higher. Bush and herb shot
upward, and some even tore themselves up
by the roots to rise more quickly. Every
native of the wood, even to the brown and
feathery rushes, grew with the rest, while
the birds ascended with the melody of
song. On a blade of grass, that fluttered
in the air like a long green ribbon, sat a
grasshopper, cleaning his wings.

"But where is the little blue flower that
grows by the water?" asked the oak, "and
the purple bell-flower and the daisy?"

"Here we are, here we are," sounded in
voice and song.

"But the beautiful thyme of last summer, where is that? and the lilies-of-the-valley, which last year covered the earth with their bloom? and the wild apple-tree, with its lovely blossoms, and all the glory of the wood, which has flourished year after year?"

"We are here, we are here," sounded voices higher in the air.

"Why this is beautiful, too beautiful to be believed," said the oak, in a joyous tone.

And the old tree, as he still grew upwards and onwards, felt that his roots were loosening themselves from the earth.

"It is right, it is best," said the tree, "no fetters hold me now. I can fly up to the very highest point in light and glory. And all I love—all are here."

Such was the dream of the old oak; and while he dreamed, a mighty storm came rushing over land and sea, at the holy Christmas time. There was a cracking and crushing heard in the tree. The root was torn from the ground just when he fancied it was being loosened from the earth. He fell—his three hundred and sixty-five years were passed as the single

day of the flies. On the morning of
Christmas-day, when the sun rose, the
storm had ceased. "The tree is down!
The old oak—our landmark on the coast!"
exclaimed the sailors.

The Little Mermaid.

THE Sea King had been a widower for many years, and his old mother kept house for him in the palace at the bottom of the sea. He had six beautiful daughters, and the youngest was the most beautiful of them all. Her skin was as clear and delicate as a rose leaf, and her eyes as blue as the deepest sea; but, like all the others, she had no feet, and her body ended in a tail, like a fish.

At last she reached her fifteenth birthday. So she said, "Farewell," and rose as lightly as a bubble to the surface of the water. The sun had just set, as she raised her head above the waves. The sea was calm, and the air mild and fresh. A large ship, with three masts, lay becalmed on the water, with only one sail set; for not a breeze stirred, and the sailors sat idle on deck or amongst the rigging. There was music and song on board; and, as darkness came on, a hundred colored lanterns were lighted, as if the flags of all nations waved in the air. The little mermaid swam close to the cabin windows; and now and then, as the waves lifted her up, she could look in through clear glass window panes, and see a number of well-dressed people within. Among them was a young prince, the most beautiful of all, with large black eyes; he was sixteen years of age, and his birthday was being kept with much rejoicing. The sailors were dancing on deck, but when the prince came out of the cabin, more than a hundred rockets rose in the air, making it as bright as day. The little mermaid was so startled that she dived under water; and when she again stretched out her head, it appeared as if all the stars of heaven were falling around her. She had never seen such fireworks before.

After a while, the sails were quickly un-

furled, and the noble ship continued her
passage; but soon the waves rose higher,
heavy clouds darkened the sky, and lightning appeared in the distance. The waves
rose mountains high, as if they would have
overtopped the mast. To the little mermaid this appeared pleasant sport; not so
to the sailors. At length the ship groaned
and creaked; the thick planks gave way
under the lashing of the sea as it broke
over the deck; the mainmast snapped asun-
der like a reed; the ship lay over on her
side, and the water rushed in. The mermaid now perceived that the crew were in
danger; even she herself was obliged to be
careful to avoid the beams and planks of
the wreck which lay scattered on the
water. At one moment it was so pitch
dark that she could not see a single object,
but a flash of lightning revealed the whole
scene; she could see every one who had
been on board excepting the prince.
When the ship parted, she had seen him
sink into the deep waves, and she was
glad, for she thought he would now be
with her; and then she remembered that

human beings could not live in the water,
so that when he got down to her father's
palace he would be quite dead. But he
must not die. So she dived deeply under
the dark waters, rising and falling with
the waves, till at length she managed to
reach the young prince. She held his head
above the water, and let the waves drift
them where they would.

In the morning the storm had ceased;
but of the ship not a single fragment
could be seen. The sun rose up red and
glowing from the water, and its beams
brought back the hue of health to the
prince's cheeks; but his eyes remained

closed. The mermaid kissed his high, smooth forehead, and stroked back his wet hair. Presently they came in sight of land. The sea here formed a little bay, in which the water was quite still, but very deep; so she swam with the handsome prince to the beach, which was covered with fine, white sand, and there she laid him in the warm sunshine. The little mermaid swam out from the shore and placed herself between some high rocks that rose out of the water; then she covered her head and neck with the foam of the sea, so that her little face might not be seen, and watched to see what would become of the poor prince. She did not wait long before she saw a young girl approach the spot where he lay. She seemed frightened at first, but only for a moment; then she fetched a number of people, and the mermaid saw that the prince came to life again, and smiled upon those who stood round him. But to her he sent no smile; he knew not that she had saved him. This made her unhappy, and when he was led away into the great building, she dived down sorrow-

fully into the water, and returned to her
father's castle. She had always been silent
and thoughtful, and now she was more so.

"If human beings are not drowned," asked
the mermaid, "can they live for ever? do
they never die as we do here in the sea?"

"Yes," replied the old lady, "they must also die, and their term of life is even shorter than ours. We sometimes live to three hundred years, but when we cease to exist here we only become the foam on the surface of the water, and we have not even a grave down here of those we love. We have not immortal souls, we shall never live again; but, like the green sea-weed, when once it has been cut off, we can never flourish more. Human beings, on the contrary, have a soul which lives for ever, after the body has been turned to dust. But if a man were to love you so much that you were more to him than his father or mother; and if all his thoughts and all his love were fixed upon you, and the priest placed his right hand in yours, and he promised to be true to you here and hereafter, then his soul would glide into your body and you would obtain a share in the future happiness of mankind.

And then the little mermaid went out from her garden, and took the road to the foaming whirlpools, behind which the sorceress lived.

"I know what you want," said the
sea witch; "it is very stupid of you,

but you shall have your way, and it
will bring you to sorrow, my pretty princess. I will prepare a draught for you,

with which you must swim to land to-
morrow before sunrise, and sit down on the
shore and drink it. Your tail will then
disappear, and shrink up into what mankind call legs; and you will feel great pain,
as if a sword were passing through you.
But all who see you will say that you are
the prettiest little human being they ever
saw. You will still have the same floating
gracefulness of movement, and no dancer
will ever tread so lightly; but at every step
you take it will feel as if you were treading
upon sharp knives, and that the blood must
flow; and you must give me your voice."

It all happened as the witch said. The
prince found her on the shore, and took
her to the palace. She was very soon
arrayed in costly robes of silk and muslin,
and was the most beautiful creature in
the palace; but she was dumb, and could
neither speak nor sing.

Finally, the prince was going to be married to the princess of a neighboring
country. When he arrived there in his ship
the church bells were ringing, and from
the high towers sounded a flourish of

trumpets; and soldiers, with flying colors and glittering bayonets, lined the roads through which they passed.

The little mermaid kissed his hand, and felt as if her heart were already broken. His wedding morning would bring death to her, and she would change into foam.

After the wedding they all went on board the ship to rest. The little mermaid leaned her white arms on the edge of the vessel, and looked towards the east for the first ray of the dawn which was to be her death. She saw her sisters rising out of the flood.

"We have given our hair to the witch," said they, "to obtain help for you, that you may not die to-night. She has given us a knife: here it is—see, it is very sharp. Before the sun rises you must plunge it into the heart of the prince; when the warm blood falls upon your feet they will grow together again, and form into a fish's tail, and you will be once more a mermaid."

The little mermaid drew back the crimson curtain of the couch, and beheld the fair bride with her head resting upon the prince's breast. She bent down and kissed

his fair brow, then looked at the sky on
which the rosy dawn grew brighter and
brighter; then she glanced at the knife,
and again fixed her eyes on the prince.
Then she threw the knife into the sea and
plunged in herself. When she opened her
eyes, she found herself surrounded by
beautiful beings like angels.

"Where am I?" asked she.

"Among the daughters of the air,"
answered one of them.

The Wild Swans.

In a far-off land dwelt a king who had
eleven sons and one daughter named Eliza.
The king loved his children dearly, and
gave them everything that children can wish
for, and they were very happy. But this
was not always to last. The king married
a new wife, for the children's mother was
dead. The new Queen hated Eliza and her
eleven brothers, and resolved to get rid of
them. She was a wicked witch, and she
said to the little princes: "Fly away like
great birds who have no voice." Then the
little princes were changed to eleven white

swans and they flew out of the palace windows and away to the forest.

Then the wicked queen rubbed Eliza's face with walnut juice and tangled her hair, so that her father did not know her, and was very cross and ugly. Only the watchdog and the swallows knew her, and they

could not speak a word. Then Eliza started from the castle to find her brothers. She reached a great wood, and soon lost her way. When night came, she lay down on the moss and cried herself to sleep. When it was morning she felt much better and resumed her journey. She came to a clear brook,

and when she saw her reflection in it, she
was horrified at her ugly appearance. When

she had bathed herself, however, she became
a beautiful little princess again.

When the sun was about to set, Eliza
saw eleven white swans with golden crowns

on their heads, flying towards the land, one behind the other, like a long white ribbon. The swans alighted quite close to her, and flapped their great white wings. As soon as the sun had disappeared under the water, the feathers of the swans fell off, and eleven beautiful princes, Eliza's brothers, stood near her. She uttered a loud cry, for, although they were very much changed, she knew them immediately. She sprang into their arms, and called them each by name. Then how happy the princes were at meeting their little sister again, for they

recognized her, although she had grown so tall and beautiful. "We brothers," said the eldest, "fly about as wild swans, so long as the sun is in the sky; but as soon as it sinks behind the hills, we recover our human shape. We do not dwell here, but in a land that lies beyond the ocean. We are permitted to visit our home once every year and to remain eleven days. To-morrow our time is up, and we must go back and remain for a whole year."

"Take me with you," begged Eliza. So they spent the whole night, weaving a strong net of rushes. In the morning Eliza placed herself upon it; the swans took it in their beaks and away they flew, till they reached the land where the swans lived, and being very tired they all went to sleep in a cave, on the floor of which the over-grown, yet delicate, green creeping plants looked like an embroidered carpet. "Now we shall expect to hear what you dream of to-night," said the youngest brother, as he showed his sister her bedroom.

"Heaven grant that I may dream how to save you," she replied. And this thought took such hold upon her mind that she prayed earnestly to God for help, and even in her sleep she continued to pray. Then it appeared to her as if she were flying high in the air, towards the cloudy palace of the "Fata Morgana," and a fairy came out to meet her, and said:

"Your brothers can be released, if you have only courage and perseverance. Do you see the stinging nettle which I hold in my hand? Quantities of the same sort grow round the cave in which you sleep, but none others will be of any use to you unless they grow upon the graves in a churchyard These you must gather even

while they burn blisters on your hands.
Break them to pieces with your hands and
feet, and they will become flax, from which
you must spin and weave eleven coats with
long sleeves; if these are then thrown over
the eleven swans, the spell will be broken.
But remember that from the moment you
commence your task until it is finished,
even should it occupy years of your life,
you must not speak. The first word you
utter will pierce through the hearts of
your brothers like a deadly dagger. Their
lives hang upon your tongue. Remember
all I have told you? And as she finished
speaking, she touched her hand lightly
with the nettle, and a pain, as of burning
fire, awoke Eliza.

When Eliza woke, it was broad daylight,
and she at once found some nettles and
began her task. One coat was finished and
the second began, when the King, who was
out hunting, found her in the cave.

"How did you come here, my sweet
child?" he asked. But Eliza shook her
head. She dared not speak, at the cost of
her brothers' lives. And she hid her hands

under her apron, so that the king might not
see how she must be suffering.

"Come with me," he said; "here you
cannot remain. If you are as good as you
are beautiful, I will dress you in silk and
velvet, I will place a golden crown on your
head, and you shall dwell, and rule, and
make your home in my richest castle."
And then he lifted her on his horse. She
wept and wrung her hands, but the king
said: "I wish only your happiness. A time
will come when you will thank me for this."
And then he galloped away over the mountains, holding her before him on his horse,
and the hunters followed behind them. On
arriving at the castle, the king led her into
marble halls, where large fountains played,
and where the walls and the ceilings were
covered with rich paintings. But she had no
eyes for all these glorious sights, she could
only mourn and weep. She had taken with
her the coat and some nettles, and she continued her work. The bishop said she was
a witch, because she did not talk, but the
King did not listen to him. She had to go
to the graveyard every night for nettles, and

finally they all came to believe the bishop, and the King consented that she should be burned.

And now all the people came to see the witch burned. An old horse drew the cart on which she sat. They had dressed her in a garment of coarse sackcloth. Her

lovely hair hung loose on her shoulders, her cheeks were deadly pale, her lips moved silently, while her fingers still worked at the green flax. Even on the way to death she would not give up her task. The ten coats of mail lay at her feet, she was working hard at the eleventh, while the mob jeered her and said: "See

the witch, how she mutters! She has no
hymn-book in her hand. She sits there
with her ugly sorcery. Let us tear it in a
thousand pieces."

And then they pressed towards her, and
would have destroyed the coats of mail,
but at the same moment eleven wild swans
flew over her, and alighted on the cart.
Then they flapped their large wings,
and the crowd drew on one side in
alarm.

As the executioner seized her by the
hand, to lift her out of the cart, she hastily
threw the eleven coats of mail over the
swans, and they immediately became eleven
handsome princes. But the youngest had a
swan's wing, instead of an arm; for she
had not been able to finish the last sleeve.

"Now I may speak," she exclaimed. "I
am innocent."

Then the people, who saw what happened, bowed to her, as before a saint; but
she sank lifeless in her brothers' arms,
overcome with suspense, anguish, and pain.

"Yes, she is innocent," said the eldest
brother; and then he related all that had

taken place; and while he spoke there
rose in the air a fragrance as from millions
of roses. Every piece of fagot in the pile
had taken root, and threw out branches,
and, above all, bloomed a white flower that
glittered like a star. This flower the king
plucked, and placed in Eliza's bosom, when
she awoke from her swoon, with peace and
happiness in her heart. And all the church
bells rang of themselves, and the birds
came in great troops. And a marriage
procession returned to the castle, such as
no king had ever before seen.

Thumbelina.

THUMBELINA was but half as big as your thumb. She was born in a tulip, and had half of a walnut shell for a cradle. Her bed was made of violet leaves, with a pink rose leaf for a counterpane. One night, as she lay sleeping, an ugly toad crept in and carried her off to make her marry her ugly son. The toad took her to her home on the bank of a stream; and to keep her safe, she swam out and placed her on a leaf of a water-lily far out in the stream, while she went to prepare a room for her.

The little fishes, who swam about in the water beneath, had seen the toad, and heard what she said, so they lifted their heads above the water to look at the little maiden. As soon as they caught sight of her, they saw she was very pretty, and it made them very sorry to think that she must go and live with the ugly toads.

"No, it must never be !" so they assembled together in the water, round the green stalk which held the leaf on which the little maiden stood, and gnawed it away at the root with their teeth. Then the leaf floated down the stream, carrying Tiny far away to other lands.

A pretty butterfly came past, and Thumbelina tied her to the leaf with her girdle, and the butterfly dragged her swiftly along. A cockchafer saw her, and seizing her around her slender waist, flew away with her to his tree. Then Thumbelina felt very sorry for the poor butterfly tied to the leaf. The cockchafer who took her away, thought Thumbelina very pretty ; but all the lady cockchafers turned up their noses and said she looked too much like a human being to be handsome. So the cockchafer flew down from the tree with her, and put her on a daisy, to let her go where she pleased.

During the whole summer poor little Tiny lived quite alone in the forest. She wove herself a bed with blades of grass, and hung it up under a broad leaf, to protect herself from the rain. She sucked the honey from the flowers for food, and drank the dew from their leaves every morning. So passed away the summer and winter— the long, cold winter. All the birds who had sung to her so sweetly were flown away, and the trees and flowers had

withered. The large clover leaf, under the shelter of which she had lived, was now rolled together and shrivelled up; nothing remained but a yellow withered stalk. She felt dreadfully cold, for her clothes were torn, and she was herself so frail and delicate, that poor little Tiny was nearly frozen to death. She came at last to the door of a field-mouse, who had a little den under the corn-stubble. There dwelt the field-mouse in warmth and comfort, with a whole roomful of corn. Poor little Tiny stood before the door just like a beggar-girl, and begged for a small piece of barley-corn, for she had been without a morsel to eat for two days.

"You poor little creature," said the field-mouse, who was really a good old field-mouse, "come into my warm room and dine with me." She was very pleased with Tiny, so she said: "You are quite welcome to stay with me all the winter, if you like; but you must keep my room clean and neat." And Tiny did all the field-mouse asked her to do, and found herself very comfortable.

An old, blind mole lived close by, and the field-mouse said Thumbelina must be his wife. One day, as they were all taking a walk in one of the dark passages of the mole, they came upon a swallow who seemed to be dead, but when Thumbelina came back to him, she found that he was only be-numbed with the cold, so she covered him

with warm wool, till he was restored. In the
spring, he flew away. He wanted Thumbelina to go with him, but she said it was
not right for her to leave the good field.
mouse. When it came winter again, she
was to marry the old mole. All summer
long she cried about it for she did not like
the mole.

One day in the fall, she sat moaning to her
self, because the wedding was near, and then
she would have to live under ground with
the mole. "Oh, that I had gone off with
the swallow," said she. "Tweet, tweet,"
came a voice just over her head, and looking
up, she saw the swallow himself. He was
probably looking for her, and how pleased
he was when he saw her! When she told
him about the coming wedding, he begged
her again to go away with him, and at last
she consented. She sat on his back and
away they went to his home far in the
south. When they came there he placed
her on a beautiful flower, which happened
to be the home of the prince of all the
flowers. When he saw Thumbelina, he
thought her the most beautiful maiden he

had ever seen, and when he asked her to marry him she willingly consented. This was much better than being the wife of a toad or a mole.

Little Claus and Big Claus.

In a village there once lived two men who were both called Claus. One of them had four horses, but the other had only one; so to distinguish them, people called the owner of the four horses, "Great Claus," and he who had only one, "Little Claus."

Through the whole week, Little Claus was obliged to plough for Great Claus, and

lent him his one horse; and once a week, on a Sunday, Great Claus lent him all his four horses. Then how Little Claus would smack his whip over all five horses and say: "Gee-up, my five horses."

"You must not say that," said Big Claus; "for only one of them belongs to you." But Little Claus would call out, "Gee-up, my five horses!"

"Now I must beg of you not to say that again," said Big Claus; "for if you do, I shall hit your horse on the head, so that he will drop dead."

"I promise you I will not say it any more," said the other; but as soon as people came by, nodding to him, and wishing him "Good day," he became so pleased that he cried out again: "Gee-up, all my horses!"

"I'll gee-up your horses for you," said Big Claus; and, seizing a hammer, he struck the one horse of Little Claus on the head, and he fell dead.

"Oh, now I have no horse at all," said Little Claus, weeping. But after a while he took off the dead horse's skin, and hung

the hide to dry in the wind. Then he put
the dry skin into a bag, and, placing it over

his shoulder, went into the next town to
sell the horse's skin.

At night, he lost his way and stopped at

a house for a lodging. But the woman said her husband was away and she shut the door in his face. Close to the house was a shed with a thatched roof, and Little Claus climbed up there for a night's sleep. From the top of the shed he could look into the window, and there he saw the woman having a grand feast with the sexton. Now, the husband hated the sexton, so this one had called while he was away. Pretty soon the husband was heard coming down the road. The woman hid the sexton in a chest, hid the wine behind the door, and the roast meat she put back into the oven.

The man heard Little Claus on the shed and he made him come down and invited him in to supper; but the woman gave them only porridge. Little Claus did not like this, so he stepped on his dried skin and it squeaked.

"What have you got in the bag?" asked the man.

"Only a conjurer,'" said Little Claus.

"And what does he say?"

"He says there is meat in the oven."

The skin squeaked again, and Little Claus said it told him that there was wine behind the door. When the man looked and found both the meat and wine, he gave Little Claus a bushel of money for the bag. Claus said he must have the chest, too, so he gave him that, and with

the money and the chest on his wheel-barrow, Little Claus went on his way. He would not let the sexton go till he gave him another bushel of money, and now that he had so much he went home.

When Great Claus asked him where he

got all his money, he said: "Why, I sold
the horse's skin." Then Great Claus took
a hammer and killed all of his four horses,
skinned them and took their skins to the
town to sell them. When the shoemakers
asked him the price, he said a bushel of
money for each. The shoemakers thought
he was making sport of them, and they
took off their aprons and belts, and beat
him out of the town.

Great Claus was very angry at Little
Claus for getting him into such a scrape.
He went home and tied Little Claus in a
bag, and started for the river to drown
him. On the way he passed a church, and
as his conscience hurt him, he stopped for
a few moments, putting down the bag in
the road, and went into the church to pray.
A little drover came along the road, driving a great herd of cattle. He was bemoan-
ing his lot, and wishing he was in heaven.
"Get into this bag," shouted Little Claus,
"and you will be there in half an hour.
I was on the way myself."

The drover let Little Claus out of the
bag and got in himself, first charging Little

Claus to take the cattle and keep them.
Great Claus came out of the church, took

the bag to the bridge and threw it into
the river. On his way back he met Little
Claus driving home his cattle.

"Hello!" said he, "didn't I drown you in the river!"

"Oh, yes!" said Little Claus, "or you thought you did."

"How did you come here, and where did you get the cattle?"

"These are sea-cattle," said Little Claus; "I found them all in the bottom of the river. It was a piece of great luck for me to be drowned."

"What a lucky fellow you are!" exclaimed Great Claus. "Do you think I should get any sea-cattle if I went down to the bottom of the river?"

"Yes, I think so," said Little Claus. "If you will go there first, and creep into a sack, I will throw you in with the greatest pleasure."

"Thank you," said Great Claus; but remember, if I do not get any sea-cattle down there I shall come up again and give you a good thrashing."

"No, now, don't be too fierce about it!" said Little Claus.

"Put in a stone," said Great Claus, "or I may not sink."

" Oh there's not much fear of that," he replied ; still he put a large stone into the bag,
and then tied it tightly, and gave it a push.

"Plump !" In went Great Claus, and
immediately sank to the bottom of the river.

The Ugly Duckling.

AN old duck was sitting on her nest,
waiting for her brood to hatch. She was
getting very tired, when one day the shells
began to crack, and one after another the
young ducks began to stick their heads out
and cry: "Peep, peep." The old duck sat
on, for the largest egg of all had not yet
hatched. "Well, how are you getting on ?"
asked an old duck, who paid her a visit.

"One egg is not hatched yet," said the
duck.

"Let me see the egg that will not break,"

said the old duck; "I have no doubt it is
a turkey's egg. I was persuaded to hatch
some once, and after all my care and trouble
with the young ones, they were afraid of
the water. Yes, that is a turkey's egg;
take my advice, leave it where it is, and
teach the other children to swim."

"I think I will sit on it a little while
longer," said the duck: "as I have sat so
long already."

"Please yourself," said the old duck, and
she went away.

At last the large egg broke, and a
young one crept forth, crying: "Peep,
peep." It was very large and ugly. The

duck stared at it, and exclaimed : "It is very large, and not at all like the others. I wonder if it really is a turkey. We shall soon find it out, however." She took them directly to the water, and the ugly duckling plunged in and swam as well as the rest.

But the little thing was so ugly that the others all fought it, and took its food away, and as it grew, its life became a burden. Finally, he could stand it no longer and he ran away and went to a moor where the wild ducks were, who treated him very well. In a few days some sportsmen came with their dogs, and there was a great fluttering among the ducks. Many of them were shot, and the ugly duckling was so frightened that he crept under some rushes and stayed all day and all night.

The next morning he resolved to leave the moor. He was very hungry, and when he came to a little cottage with the door a little open he went in. An old woman and a cat and a hen lived in the cottage. The old woman seemed glad to see him, and gave him some food directly, and he sat

down in the corner, quite contented. In a
few days he felt a longing for a swim in
the cool water. He mentioned it to the

cat and the hen, and they laughed at him.
"Did you ever hear of such a thing?" said
they; "he must be crazy."

But one morning when nobody was
looking the duckling crept slyly out of the

door and started to look for a pond or a
river. As he flapped his wings, he was
surprised to feel how strong they were.

Some beautiful birds flew over his head, and he longed to go with them. They were swans, but he did not know that, and he had never felt so strange a liking for any other birds. He flapped his wings again, and almost before he knew it he was sailing through the air. He flew till he came to a large pond in a garden, where he saw some of the beautiful birds with the long necks swimming. He lit on the water right among them. He thought they would surely fight him like the ducks, but they didn't; they came around him with every manifestation of joy. Some little children clapped their hands and cried: "Oh, here is a new swan."

Thick-headed Jack.

A RICH country squire had two sons, who both wished to marry the king's daughter. She had given out publicly that she would marry the man who could give the readiest answer. One of the brothers knew the

Latin dictionary by heart, and the other
knew all about law. Their father gave each
of them a beautiful horse, and they set out
to the house of the princess. Just as they
were starting, the youngest brother came up.
He was never counted with his brothers
because he was so dull. He was called
Thick-headed Jack.

"Hallo!" cried Jack; "where are you
off to?"

"To the king's palace. Don't you know
what all the world knows?" and they told
him the whole story.

"My gracious! I shall come too," cried
he. The brothers laughed scornfully and
rode away.

"Daddy," cried Jack, "I must have a
horse. If you only knew what a hurry I'm
in to get married!"

"Hold your foolish tongue!" cried his
father. "You shall have no horse. *You*
can't phrase your words properly. You
and your brothers are different beings."

"Well," cried Jack, "if I can't have a
horse, I'll take the old goat. It belongs to
me." So said, so done. He mounted the

old goat, and off he was down the turnpike road like a storm wind.

His brothers were riding slowly; neither spoke, lest he should forget the things he had learned to say to the princess.

"Hallo !" cried Thick-headed Jack, "I'm coming. Just look what I've found on the road !" and he showed them a dead crow.

"Blockhead !" cried his brothers. "What are you going to do with that ?"

"Going to give it to the princess."

"You had better !" said his brothers.

"Hallo ! Look what I have found now."

"Blockhead !" they cried; "it is nothing but an old wooden shoe. Are you going to give that to the princess ?"

"Perhaps I may," said Thick-headed Jack. The brothers laughed and rode on; they were now a long way in advance. "Hoppity-hop ! Here I come !" cried Jack. "Look here, better and better !"

"What have you got now?" asked the brothers.

"Oh, I could not tell you," cried Thick-headed Jack; "it is *too* grand !"

"Oh, fie !" cried the brothers; "why, that

is mud, nothing but mud out of the gutter."

"So it is," cried Jack; "the very finest sort;" and he filled his pocket with the mud.

The brothers galloped away till the sparks flew right and left; they reached the town-gate earlier than Thick-headed Jack.

All the people of the land stood in crowds round the palace windows to see the princess receive her suitors. As soon as any of them entered the hall where she was, his speech went out like a candle.

"He is no good," cried the king's daughter; "out with him!"

At last it came to the turn of the brother who knew the Latin dictionary, but he had forgotten every word.

"It's awfully hot here," said he.

"Yes, indeed; but my father is roasting some chickens to-day."

"Ahem! ahem!" There he stood like a simpleton. He had never expected such a conversation as this; and he had not a word to say. He would have liked to say something very witty—"Ahem!"

"He is no good," said the king's

daughter. "Out with him." And out he
had to go. The other brother came in.

"It's awfully hot here," he said.
"Yes, indeed; we are roasting chickens."
"How—do—how?" he began.

"He is no good," said the king's daughter; "send him away." Then came Thick-headed Jack, galloping, goat and all, straight into the room. "Puff! it's murdering hot," he cried.

"Yes, indeed; but my father is roasting chickens to-day."

"Oh! then I can roast my crow," said Thick-headed Jack

"With pleasure," said the princess. "But have you anything to roast it in?"

"I have, though," said Jack. "Here is a cooking utensil." He took out the old wooden shoe and put the crow inside it

"That is a regular meal," said the princess; "but where shall we get soup?"

"I've got that in my pocket," said Jack. "I've enough and to spare," and he threw some mud on the floor.

"Now, I like that," said the princess. "You have an answer ready, and you can speak. I choose you for my husband, and the rest may all go home."

So Thick-headed Jack was made king, and sat on a throne. He won a crown and a wife, and all by having an answer ready.

The Brave Tin Soldier.

THERE were once five-and-twenty tin soldiers, who were all brothers, for they had been made out of the same old tin spoon. They shouldered arms and looked straight before them, and wore a splendid uniform, red and blue. The first thing in the world they ever heard were the words, "Tin soldiers!" uttered by a little boy, who clapped his hands with delight when the lid of the box, in which they lay, was taken off. The soldiers were all exactly alike, excepting one, who had only one leg; he had been left to the last, and then there was not enough tin to finish him, so they made him to stand firmly on one leg.

The table was covered with other playthings, but the prettiest of all was a tiny little lady made of paper. She was a dancer, and she stretched out both her arms, and raised one of her legs so high, that the tin soldier thought that she, like himself, had only one leg. "That is the wife for me," he thought. Then he laid himself behind the snuff-box, so he could peep at the little lady. When evening came, the people of the house went to bed. Then the playthings began to have their own games together, to pay visits, to have sham fights, and to give balls. The nutcrackers played at leap-frog, and the pencil jumped about the table. Only the tin soldier and the dancer remained in their places. She stood on tip-toe, with her arms stretched out, as firmly as he did on his one leg. The clock struck twelve, and,

with a bounce, up sprang the lid of the
snuff-box; but, instead of snuff, there jumped
up a little black goblin.

"Tin soldier," said the goblin, "don't
wish for what does not belong to you."

When the children came in the next
morning, they placed the tin soldier in the

window. Now, whether it was the goblin
who did it, or the draught, is not known,
but the window flew open, and out fell
the tin soldier, heels over head, from the
third story, into the street beneath. It
was a terrible fall; for he came head
downwards, his helmet and his bayonet
stuck in between the flagstones, and his

one leg up in the air. The servant-maid and the little boy went downstairs directly to look for him; but he was nowhere to be seen, although once they nearly trod upon him.

Presently there was a heavy shower. When it was over, two boys happened to pass by, and one of them said, " Look, there is a tin soldier. He ought to have a boat to sail in."

So they made a boat out of a newspaper, and placed the tin soldier in it, and sent him sailing down the gutter, while the two boys ran by the side of it, and clapped their hands. Good gracious, what large waves arose in that gutter! and how fast the stream rolled on! The paper boat rocked up and down, and turned itself round sometimes so quickly that the tin soldier trembled; yet he remained firm; his countenance did not change; he looked straight before, and shouldered his musket. Suddenly the boat shot under the bridge which formed part of a drain, and then it was as dark as the tin soldier's box.

"Where am I going now?" thought he.

Suddenly there appeared a great water-rat, who lived in the drain.

"Have you a passport?" asked the rat; "give it to me at once." But the tin sol-

dier remained silent and held his musket tighter than ever. The boat sailed on and the stream rushed on stronger and stronger. The tin soldier could already see daylight

shining where the arch ended. Then he
heard a roaring sound. At the end of the
tunnel the drain fell into a large canal over
a steep place. The boat rushed on, and
the poor tin soldier held himself as stiffly
as possible, without moving an eyelid.

Then the boat fell to pieces, and the
soldier was swallowed by a great fish,
which was caught, taken to the market
and sold to the cook. She cut him open
and cried out: "Oh, here is the tin soldier" She took him into the same room,
and there was the elegant little dancer still
balancing herself on one leg, and everything
was just as he had left it.

The Nightingale.

A LONG time ago the emperor of China
had a beautiful palace, built entirely of
porcelain. It was so delicate and brittle
that whoever touched it had to take care.
All about it was a garden filled with the
rarest flowers. The garden extended so
far that even the gardener himself did not
know where it stopped. But the fisher-
men knew that beyond it was a noble
forest sloping down to the sea, and that in
one of the trees lived a nightingale that
sang sweetly to them every night.

Strangers came to China from all parts
of the world, and when they went home

they wrote books, describing all the beautiful things; but they all ended by saying: "The nightingale is the most beautiful of all." One of these books fell into the emperor's hands. He was much pleased with all the praises; but when he came to the part telling of the nightingale, he was much surprised. "What is this?" said he. "Have I such a bird in my empire? I have never heard of it."

Then he called one of his lords-in-waiting.

"There is a very wonderful bird mentioned here, called a nightingale," said the emperor; "they say it is the best thing in my large kingdom. Why have I not been told of it?"

"I have never heard the name," replied the cavalier; "she has not been presented at court."

"It is my pleasure that she shall appear this evening," said the emperor.

But where was the nightingale to be found? The nobleman went upstairs and down, through halls and passages; yet none of those whom he met had heard of the bird.

"But I will hear the nightingale." said the emperor; "she must be here this evening; and if she does not come the whole court shall be trampled upon after supper is ended."

"Tsing-pe!" cried the lord-in-waiting, and again he ran up and down stairs; and half the court ran with him, for they did not like the idea of being trampled upon.

At last they met with a poor little girl

in the kitchen, who said: "Oh, yes, I know the nightingale quite well."

"Little maiden," said the lord-in-waiting, you shall have permission to see the emperor dine, if you will lead us to the nightingale." So she went into the wood, and half the court followed her.

"Hark, hark! there she is," said the girl.

"Is it possible?" said the lord-in-waiting; "I never imagined it would be a little, plain, simple thing like that."

"My excellent little nightingle," said the courtier, "I have the great pleasure of inviting you to a court festival this evening, where you will gain imperial favor by your charming song."

"My song sounds best in the green wood," said the bird; but still she came willingly.

The palace was elegantly decorated for the occasion. The walls and floors of porcelain glittered in the light of a thousand lamps. Beautiful flowers, round which little bells were tied, stood in the corridors: what with the running to and fro and the draught, these bells tinkled so loudly that no one could speak to be heard. In the centre of the great hall, a golden perch had been fixed for the nightingale to sit on. The whole court was present, and the little kitchen-maid had received permission to stand by the door. The nightingale sang so sweetly that the tears came into the emperor's eyes; and then rolled down his cheeks, as her song became still more touching and went to every one's heart. The emperor was so delighted that he declared the nightingale should have his gold slipper to wear round her neck, but she declined the honor with thanks; she had been sufficiently rewarded already. " I have seen tears in an emperor's eyes," she said; "that is my richest reward."

Now, the whole city rang with praises of the bird. Everybody talked of her. She was put in a golden cage, and was allowed to fly out every day, accompanied by twelve ladies-in-waiting who held silken cords attached to her feet. One day the emperor received from Japan a present of a golden bird that was covered with dia-

monds and gems. It was made to wind
up like a clock, and then it would sing
like the nightingale. They all said it
sang better than the nightingale; but an
old fisherman said its song was very
pretty, but it lacked something—he could
not tell what.

The emperor and the court now fell in
love with the new golden bird, and the nightingale was allowed to fly away out of the
window. One evening, when the artificial
bird was singing its best, something inside
sounded "whizz." Then a spring cracked.
"Whir-r-r-r" went all the wheels, and then
the music stopped. The emperor immediately called for his physician; but what
could he do? Then they sent for a watch-
maker; and, after a great deal of talking
the bird was put into something like
order; but he said that it must be used
very carefully. Now there was great
sorrow, as the bird could only be allowed
to play once a year, and even that was
dangerous for the works inside.

Five years passed, and then a real grief
came upon the land. Cold and pale lay

the emperor in his royal bed; the whole
court thought he was dead, and every one
ran away to pay homage to his successor.
But the emperor was not yet dead. A
window stood open, and the moon shone
in upon the artificial bird. The poor
emperor, finding he could scarcely breathe
with a strange weight on his chest, opened
his eyes, and saw Death sitting there. All
around the bed were a number of strange
heads, some very ugly, and others lovely
and gentle-looking. These were the emperor's good and bad deeds, which stared
him in the face.

"Sing," said the emperor to the golden
bird, "and drive these horrid things away."
But how could the golden thing sing, when
there was no one to wind it? Then came
through the window the beautiful song
of the nightingale, who had come back to
sing to the king. He sang till Death flew
out of the window, and the king, now
quite recovered, got up and walked about
his chamber. When the courtiers came in
to find him dead, he bade them "Good
morning!"

The Swineherd.

THERE was once a young prince who had a small kingdom, and a very little money. Yet he was bold enough to want to marry the emperor's daughter. In the prince's garden grew a rose tree of a most unusual kind, which bore flowers but once in five years; and then only one rose. But the fragrance of this one rose was so sweet that people who inhaled it forgot for the time all their cares and sorrows. Besides this rose-tree the prince had a nightingale that sang so sweetly, it seemed as if all the

loveliest melodies were seated in its throat.
The flower-tree and the bird were both
packed carefully in large silver vases, and
forwarded to the princess, who, when she
saw them, clapped her hands with joy,
exclaiming: "Oh, suppose there should be
a little pussy-cat for me!"

When she saw the rose-tree, she turned
away, and said : "It is only a natural rose-
tree;" and when the bird was taken out
in his cage, she was displeased, because it
was only a natural bird. When the prince
found that his presents were not accepted,
he stained his face brown, and his hair
black, put on some old clothes, pulled his
hat down low, and went to the emperor's
palace, and engaged to be swineherd to the
emperor. He lived in a little room close
to the pig-sties, and watched the pigs all
day.

But while he was watching the pigs, he
made a pretty little kettle, hung about
with bells. And when the kettle boiled,
the bells would play a tune. But this was
not all; whoever put his finger in the
steam, could tell just what everybody was

having for breakfast. It was a wonderful kettle.

When the princess went to walk with
her maids, she heard the kettle playing, and
she wanted to buy it. The disguised
prince said she might have it for ten
kisses.

The princess was offended at the pre-
sumption of the swineherd, and she turned
to walk away. But the kettle began to
sing again, and she turned back, and
bought it, giving the swineherd ten kisses,
with the maids all standing around, so
that no one should see. They took the
kettle away, and found much pleasure in
hearing it sing, and finding out what their
neighbors were cooking for breakfast.

The swineherd then made a wonderful
musical rattle, that played all the tunes
that ever were made. When the princess
heard it, she wanted the rattle also, but
the swineherd would not give it to her for
less than a hundred kisses. "I must have
the rattle," said the princess. "Take your
places and form a ring round me." So the
ladies quickly formed a circle round the

princess, and spread out their dresses to hide her.

"What can all that commotion be about,

near the pigsties?" asked the emperor, as he came out on the high balcony. Then he rubbed his eyes and put on his spectacles.

"It looks as if the ladies of the court were having some foolish frolic; I must go nearer and see what it means." So he pulled up his slippers and walked slowly and cautiously through the garden, but the ladies were so busy counting the kisses, that they did not notice the emperor's approach, till he came so close that he stood on tiptoe to see what was going on.

"What is all this?" he asked, and the next moment, when he saw the kissing going on, he drew off his slipper and threw it at the head of the swineherd.

"Pack yourselves off quickly, bag and baggage," he thundered.

"Oh, wretched creature that I am," sighed the princess; "if I had only accepted the offer of that handsome prince I would not now be in so miserable a plight!"

Then the swineherd stepped behind a tree, put on his princely dress, and came out looking so handsome that the princess curtsied to him, and said at once she would marry him. But the prince turned his back on her, saying: "You refused the

offer of an honorable prince, and for
trifling toys have permitted yourself to be
kissed by a swineherd." And he would
have nothing more to do with her.

The Ice Maiden.

LITTLE RUDY lived in a pretty valley of
the Alps. It is on these mountains that
the Ice Maiden lives, she of whom the old
people talk in whispers, for she does not
like men, and she lies in wait for them in
the clefts and on the high peaks. She
builds for herself great palaces that glisten
in the sun, and sometimes show all the
colors of the rainbow. She piles the snow
high in the passes and sometimes sends it
sliding down the sides of the mountain.
Then the people turn white with fear, and
say the avalanche is coming.

But Rudy was not afraid of the Ice
Maiden. He clambered about the mountain peaks like the chamois, who were more
afraid of him than of the older hunters for
he was a good shot, and he could climb
nearer to them when they thought themselves in safe places.

When Rudy was a very little boy, his
mother started with him in her arms to
visit his grandfather over the mountain. It
had been snowing for several days and

now the snow lay deep on the ledges. In crossing one of these the snow gave way and she and Rudy fell into a cleft. When they were taken out Rudy was alive, but his mother was dead.

As Rudy grew older, all the maidens were in love with him, but he had eyes only for one—the miller's daughter, Babette. So bold and handsome a lad was not to be refused, so when he asked her to marry him, she blushed and consented. They went to Villeneuve to be married, and while Babette's father took his after-dinner nap, they rowed on the lake to a little island. As they sat on the shore, a sudden storm of wind arose and the boat broke her mooring and was fast drifting. Rudy was a good swimmer, and he jumped into the lake and swam for the boat. The Ice Maiden kissed him as he swam, and he grew stiff with cold and sank. As Babette watched for him on the shore, the lightning flashed, and she saw his body, and the Ice Maiden stood with one foot pressing him down, and so they floated out of her sight.

The Marsh King's Daughter.

THE storks tell to their young ones many a story, which are almost always tales of the moorland and the sedge; and they are always adapted to the age of the listener. The very youngest are satisfied if they hear "Kribble-krabble-plurry-murry;" they think that is very nice; but the elder ones like something with a deeper meaning, or a fragment of family history. One of the very oldest stories told by the storks is known to us all; it is that of Moses lying among the reeds on the banks

of the Nile. The second is not nearly so
widely known. It has been handed down
for thousands of years from mother stork
to mother stork.

The first pair of storks who brought
over the story, and were mixed up in it

themselves, had their summer residence in
the Viking's palace on the moorland in
Wendyssel, at the northern point of Jut-
land. The place is still a vast, desolate
moor, and whatever attempts to pass over
it sinks out of sight.

One evening the father stork stayed out

very late, and when he came home he said
he had seen the princess whom they knew
in Egypt. He had been to the moor, and,
he said, " the princess came there with two
of her maids, all in the shape of swans.
The princess took off her swan's dress,
and gave it to her maids to hold while she
looked for a flower which grew there, and
which she said was the only thing that
would cure her sick father in Egypt. The
maids tore the robe into pieces and flew
away.

"The princess cried aloud, and her tears
fell on the alder stump. It was no common alder; it was the marsh king himself,
who reigns over the whole moor. I saw
him stretch out his knotty arms like long,
shining branches, and clutch at the princess. The poor child fled from him in
terror; she sped along the green, shaking
bog; but the ground would not bear my
weight, much less hers, and I saw her sink
below the fen, and the alder stump followed her and dragged her down. Black
bubbles rose from the marsh, and then
every trace of them had vanished. The

princess lies buried in the marsh, and will never bring a flower to Egypt. It would have broken your heart, little mother, if you had seen it.

" I shall go there every day to see if any-thing comes of it," said the father stork; and so he did.

A long time passed away, and then the stork saw a stem rise from the pond. When it had pierced the surface of the water, it unfolded into a cluster of leaves, with one large bud in the centre. The stork flew over the pond and saw the bud open under the burning sun; inside the flower lay a lovely little baby, as fresh and bright as if it had just left its bath. It looked so like the Egyptian princess, that for a moment the stork thought that it must be she; but when he had taken time to reflect, he decided that it was the child of the princess and the marsh king who lay sleeping in the water-lily.

"She cannot possibly stay here," said the father stork; and there are too many of us already in the nest. Stay! I know what I will do with her. The Viking's wife has no children; she has often longed for a little one, and I hear them say the stork will

bring one some day. I will take them at their word. How delighted they will all be!"

The stork lifted the little creature from the lily, flew to the Viking's palace, and laid the baby in the lap of the Viking's wife.

The Viking's wife was delighted with the little baby. She kissed it and caressed it, but the little thing fought her, and scratched her, and was as wild as a tiger. At last it cried itself to sleep; then night came and the Viking's wife folded her in her arms and went to sleep too. In the night she awoke and missed her baby. She hunted all over the bed but could not find it. At the foot of the bed, however, lay an ugly green frog. The Viking's wife was about to throw it outdoors, but it looked at her so pitifully that she let it remain. In the morning, the frog was gone, but in its place lay the beautiful, cross baby. The Viking's wife learned the secret. In the daytime the child looked like its mother, but had the ugly disposition of its father, the marsh king; in the night it changed to a frog, but had the lovely disposition of the princess. The Viking was away, and his wife determined not to tell him about it,

but to let him see the child only in the day
time. So the child grew to be a beautiful
maiden, but so wild that she made the
Viking's wife a great deal of trouble.

The storks had been to Egypt many
times. The young storks were grown and
they had delightful times on the Nile But
in the palace there was no pleasure. The
two maids had come back and treacherously

told that the young princess had been shot
by a bowman. The master lay stiff and
helpless, waiting for the magic flower that
alone could cure him.

The little girl at the Viking's house had
been named Helga. As she grew older, she
seemed to get wilder; only as evening ap
proached was she to be reasoned with, and
when the sun had set, and her form had
changed, she would sit cowering in the
shadow. Her body was much larger than
that of the largest frog, and all the more
hideous because of its size. She looked
like a misshapen dwarf with a frog's head
and webbed fingers. Her eyes were very
sorrowful, and her voice was like the inar-
ticulate sobbing of a child in its sleep. The
Viking's wife would take her on her knees,
forgetting her ugly shape; and, looking into
her piteous eyes, she often said: "I almost
wish you would stay always in your present form. My silent frog-child is not so
terrible as the beautiful girl I see by day."

The Viking returned from one of his
many warlike excursions, and brought with
him, as a prisoner, a young Christian priest.

Helga heard them tell how they were going to put him to death, and she thought it would be sport to see them. But when it came night, and she had become a frog, she felt sorry for the poor priest. She

crept to the dungeon where he lay, cut his bonds, and hopped away to the stable and showed him a fleet horse. He leaped upon the horse, took the frog in front of him and galloped away. As soon as the sun rose, the priest was astonished to see the frog changed to a beautiful maiden, who jumped from the horse and tried to run away. Fearing witchcraft, he offered a prayer and made the sign of the cross, and immediately Helga was subdued.

There was a fierce struggle going on in Helga's heart, but the priest prayed until the spell was broken and she became as gentle as a lamb. Then he took her again on the horse, but he made her ride behind him, and they galloped on. Towards evening they fell in with a band of robbers who killed the priest and took Helga with them away off toward the moor.

But when the sun set the spell returned and Helga was changed to a frog. The robbers thought she had run away and they went in search of her, leaving the frog to hop away into the bushes unmolested. The Christian's prayers were sunk deep into her heart, and she sat and sobbed all through the night. At last she prayed herself that she might have her nature changed, and a great peace came into her soul. Then the sun arose, and

the dead priest appeared to her, sitting
on his horse, with a cross in his hand.

"Child of clay," said the Christian

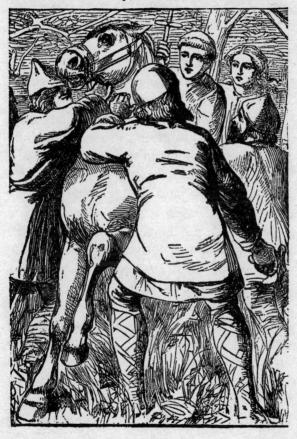

priest, "thou wast made of the dust of the earth, and from that dust thou shalt one day rise again. The light within thee is a ray from God Himself, and aspires back to its source. I am come from the land of death. I cannot lead thee to Hedebei to receive Christian baptism until thou hast drawn from the pond on the moor the living root of thy being." He raised her on the horse and placed in her hand a golden censer; a cloud of richest incense rose from it, and the wounds in the forehead of the priest shone like a wreath of stars. He lifted the cross, and the horse started away through the forest.

On sped the horse, across marsh and moor and swamp, towards the lonely pond. The priest lifted the cross; it shone like gold. He sang aloud his litanies, and fair Helga joined her voice with his, as a child tries to falter out the hymns which its mother sings; she swung the golden censer to and fro, and every rush and reed broke out into blossom; a host of water-lilies rose to the surface of the desolate pond, and lay there like a gauzy veil of blossom; the

hidden life in every seed and bud broke forth in flowers, and, stretched out along the pure, white petals, lay a sleeping woman, young and fair. Helga looked into the sleeping face, and thought for a moment that it was her own reflection in the water; but it was her mother whom she saw, the Egyptian princess from the shores of the Nile.

The priest lifted up the sleeping form on to the horse, but the phantom steed sank under the weight, as if his body were but a cere-cloth floating in the wind. The sign of the cross was traced above it, and the airy shape grew strong, and bore its triple load away from the fen to the dry land.

As they touched the shore the cock crowed; the phantoms melted away; but the mother and child stood face to face.

"Is it I myself who look out from the waters?" cried the mother.

"Is it I myself who rise from the green sedge?" said Helga.

And in a moment mother and child lay clasped in each other's arms.

Just then the old father stork appeared in the reeds, with two swan's ropes which he laid at their feet. With much clapping of his beak he told them what he had heard the two lying princesses say to the king lying sick by the Nile, and how he could not be satisfied until he had punished them;

so he stole their swan's dresses, and he and his sons had brought them all the way from Egypt. The mother and daughters soon put on the robes and went sailing away through the air.

Helga was sadly missed by the Viking's wife, who thought of her night and day.

One night she dreamed that Helga was in her frog-like shape and she held her on her knee.

She pressed a kiss on Helga's forehead, and the hideous disguise fell away; Helga stood before her in all her beauty, sweet, gentle, and loving. She kissed her foster-mother's hands, thanked and blessed her for all her love and sorrow. "The Christ has conquered," she said, and then she rose up like a stately swan, spread her white wings, and flew away.

The Viking's wife awoke at the sound of the fluttering wings. She hurried to the window and saw the flocks of storks circling round the palace turrets. Opposite the place where she stood, and just over the well where Helga's wilful ways had so often filled her heart with dread, two white swans lingered and looked back at her with mild, loving eyes.

The swans bent their necks, as if in greeting; the Viking's wife spread out her arms and smiled, with tears in her eyes.

Then, with much clapping of beaks and rustling of wings, the whole army of storks and swans turned southward and flew away.

There was great rejoicing when the princess and Helga arrived in Egypt, where the storks visited them every year.

The Emperor's New Clothes.

MANY years ago, there was an emperor who had a new suit of clothes for every hour. He cared nothing for anything but new clothes. On a certain day two men arrived in the town and gave out that they were weavers, and that they had a most wonderful fabric, that was so fine that it could not be seen by any one who was stupid or who was not fit for his position.

The emperor sent for them to weave and make him a suit of clothes of the wonderful cloth, for, said he, it will show me who are unfit among my officers. So the two men set up their looms and they worked away at them when anyone was near; but they worked in the air, for there was nothing at all in the looms.

The emperor sent in his prime minister to look at the cloth. The two rogues were very polite ; they wished him to step nearer, and inquired whether he did not think the pattern very pretty and the colors brilliant.

" Good gracious !" he said to himself, " am I becoming stupid or unfit for my position ?"

"Now what do you think of our work ?" asked the two weavers.

" Oh, it is beautiful, lovely," said the bewildered old gentleman, looking through his spectacles. " I shall tell the emperor I approve of all I have seen very much."

After this the impostors applied for money in advance and more gold and silken thread, which they readily obtained, and stowed away in a box. Then they continued their pretended work at the looms, but not a single thread was used.

The emperor soon after sent another statesman to see how the weaving was going on, and to inquire whether the stuff would soon be ready. But it was exactly the same with him as with the first. He

almost made himself half blind with
looking; but as there was nothing on
the looms, he could see nothing. "I am
not stupid," said the man to himself; "I

suppose, therefore, I am not fitted for my
situation. That, however, is a ridiculous
idea, but I must not say a word about it to
anyone." So he praised the tissue he could
not see. "It is really lovely," he said.

Everyone in the city talked about the beautiful fabric, and then the emperor expressed a wish to see for himself what this wonderful stuff was like. He approached the looms at which the two artful impostors were working with all their might, although there was not a single thread on the looms. "How is this?" said the emperor to himself. "I can see nothing; this is really dreadful. Am I stupid? Am I, as emperor, unfit for my position? It would be the most dreadful thing if that could happen to me. Oh, really, it is very beautiful," he said, aloud; "it merits my highest approval."

The whole suite who were with him looked, and looked, and could make no more of it than the others, but they said after the emperor: "Yes, it is very pretty." They advised him to wear the magnificent dress for the first time in the great procession which was about to take place.

The whole night through, before the day when the procession was to take place, the two swindlers were up and stirring. They had lighted sixteen candles, and all

the townspeople could see how hard they
were working to finish the emperor's new
clothes. They pretended to take the cloth
down from the looms, they cut with great
scissors in the air, they sewed with needles
which had no thread in them, and at last
they said : "The clothes are ready." The
emperor came himself with his most dis-
tinguished nobles; and the swindlers lifted
up one arm high in the air as if they were
holding something, and said: "Look! here
are the trousers, here is the coat, here is
the mantle!" and so on. "It is as light
and fine as cobweb; one would think one
had nothing on, but that is just the beauty
of it! May it please your imperial
majesty graciously to take off your
clothes," said the swindlers, "and we will
put on your new ones here before the large
mirror."

The emperor took off all his clothes, and
the swindlers pretended to put on each
separate article of the newly-finished suit,
while the emperor twisted and twirled
about before the mirror. "How beautifully
they fit!" exclaimed everybody, "What

a splendid fit ! What a pattern, and what colors ! ! "

"They are waiting outside with the canopy which is to be held over your majesty in the procession," announced the master of the ceremonies. " I am ready ! " said the emperor. "Doesn't it fit well ? " and then he turned once more to the look-ing-glass, as if he were carefully examining his new costume. The chamberlains who were to bear his train pretended to lift up something from the floor. So the emperor walked in procession under the splendid canopy, and all the crowd, in the street and at the windows, exclaimed: " Look how incomparably beautiful the emperor's new clothes are ! What a train he has ! and ow extremely well they fit." No one would allow it for a moment that he could see nothing at all, for then he must either be considered stupid or unfit for his office. " But he has nothing on !" cried a little child at last. " Just listen to this little innocent," said its father ; and one whispered to an-other what the child had said. " But he has nothing on !" shouted all the people at last.

"Look at the emperor with no clothes on! How ridiculous he appears!"

The emperor began to think the people were right, but he said to himself: "I must go through the procession, just as though I had."

So the pages still pretended to carry the emperor's train, although they knew there was no train to carry. And the emperor marched along to the end as though he was wonderfully dressed.

The Tinder Box.

A SOLDIER went marching by along the road. "Left, right, left, right!" He had his knapsack on his back, and a sabre at his side, for he was coming home from the war.

On the high road he met an old witch;
she was very repulsive to look at; her
under lip hung down over her chin.
"Good evening, soldier," she said. "What
a fine sabre you have got! and what a
large knapsack! You are something like
a soldier, and you shall have as much
money as ever you like."

"Thank you, old witch," said the soldier.

"Do you see that tall tree yonder?" said
the witch. "It is hollow inside. Climb
up to the top and you will see a hole
through which you can let yourself right
down into the tree. I will tie a rope round
you, so that I can pull you up when you
call to me."

"What am I to do when I am down in
the tree?" the soldier asked.

"Fetch up money," said the witch.
"Below the roots of the tree you will find
a large hall, lighted up with more than
three hundred lamps. Then you will see
three doors; open them all, the key is in
each lock. In the first room you will see
a large chest in the middle of the floor,

and on the chest a dog with eyes as big as
saucers. Don't mind him in the least.
Here is my blue-checked apron; spread
that out on the floor and put the dog upon
it, then open the chest and take out as
much copper as you like. If you prefer
silver you must go on into the next room.
But *there* is a dog with eyes as big as mill-
wheels—you need not fear him, however.
Put him on my apron and take out the
money. If you want gold, you can have
it, as much as ever you can carry, by going
into the third room ; but the dog on the
chest of gold has eyes as big as steeples—
he is a savage brute, you may take my
word for it. Never fear him, however;
put him on my apron, he won't hurt you,
and you can take as much gold as you will."

"That doesn't sound amiss," said the
soldier. "But what am I to give you for
it, old witch? for I don't suppose you
mean to do it for nothing."

"I do," said the witch. "I won't take
a penny All I ask is that you shall bring
me up an old tinder-box that my grand-
mother left the last time she was there."

"Well, then," said the soldier, "tie the rope round my waist."

"Here it is," said the witch, "and here is my blue-checked apron."

The soldier climbed up the tree, let himself down, and stood, as the witch had said, in a great hall where hundreds of lamps were burning. He opened the first door. Ugh! there sat the dog with eyes as big as saucers, glaring at him. "You're a nice fellow!" said the soldier, lifting him on to the witch's apron.

Then he filled his pockets with copper, shut the chest, and went into the next room. Right enough, there sat the dog with eyes as big as mill-wheels.

"You had better not stare so," said the soldier; "your eyes might come out of your head altogether." He lifted the dog on to the witch's apron and at the sight of all the silver in the chest, he emptied his pockets again and filled them and his knapsack too with silver. Then he went into the third room. That really was awful! The dog had eyes every inch as big as towers, and they turned round and round in his head like wheels.

"Good morning," said the soldier, touching his cap, for he had never seen such a dog in his life. But after looking at him more closely, he thought he had been civil enough, so he placed him on the floor and opened the chest. Good gracious, what a quantity of gold there was! enough to buy all the sugar-sticks of the sweet-stuff women; all the tin-soldiers, whips, and rocking-horses in the world, or even the whole town itself. There was, indeed, an immense quantity. So the soldier now threw away all the silver money he had taken, and filled his pockets and his knapsack with gold instead; and not only his pockets and his knapsack, but even his cap and his boots, so that he could scarcely walk.

He was really rich now; so he replaced the dog on the chest, closed the door, and called up through the tree, "Now pull me out, you old witch."

"Have you got the tinder-box?" asked the witch.

"No; I declare I quite forgot it." So he went back and fetched the tinder-box, and then the witch drew him up out of the tree, and he stood again in the high road, with his pockets, his knapsack, his cap, and his boots full of gold.

"What are you going to do with the tinder-box?" asked the soldier.

"That's no business of yours," said the witch; "give me the box."

"What's that you say?" cried the soldier. "Tell me this very minute what you want it for, or I'll draw my sword and cut off your head."

"I won't!" said the witch.

The soldier immediately cut off her head. There she lay. He tied up all his money in her apron, slung it like a bundle over his shoulder, put the tinder-box in his pocket, and walked on towards the town.

It was a splendid town. The soldier went into one of the best hotels, engaged

the largest room, and ordered everything
he liked best for supper. He was rich
now, because he had so much money.

The man who blacked his boots thought
it was strange that such a rich gentleman
should wear such very old boots, but the
next day the soldier bought new ones,
and a new suit of clothes. He was not a
soldier now, but a fine gentleman; and the
people spoke to him of all the remarkable
things in the town, of the king, and the
beautiful young princess, his daughter.

"Where can one see her?" asked the
soldier.

"You cannot see her," was the reply;
"she lives in a large brazen castle, surrounded by walls and turrets. No one but
the king may enter, because it was once
prophesied that she would marry a common
soldier."

"I should like to look at her," said the
soldier; but it was quite impossible for
him to obtain permission.

From this time he lived a merry life,
going to theatres, and driving about in the
royal parks and gardens. He gave away a

great deal to the poor, and that was right
of him; he knew of old what it is not to
have a shilling in one's pocket. Now he
was rich, wore fine clothes, and had num-
bers of friends, who all said he was an excellent fellow, and a perfect gentleman.
The soldier was pleased at that. But un-
luckily, as he went on spending money
every day, and never earning any more, he
found himself at last with scarcely any
left, and was obliged to leave his beautiful
rooms for a little garret under the roof.
where he had to black his own boots, and
mend them with a packing-needle. None
of his friends came to see him now—there
were too many steps to climb.

It was a dark night, and he could not
even buy himself a candle; but it suddenly occurred to him that there was a
piece of candle left in the tinder-box which
he had fetched up for the old witch, out of
the hollow tree. He struck a light, and
the moment it flashed up, the door opened,
and in came the dog with eyes as big as
saucers. "What does my lord require?"
said the dog.

"What is this?" said the soldier. "This is a lively sort of a tinder-box if I can get whatever I like out of it! Get me some money," he said to the dog, and *whish!* off he was—*whish!* there he was back again with a bag full of copper, in his mouth.

Then the soldier began to see what a famous box it was. You struck it once, and up came the dog with eyes as big as saucers; you struck it twice, and up came the one that sat on the chest of silver; three times, and up came the one that kept guard over the gold. The soldier went down stairs again into his beautiful rooms, and bought some more fine clothes. Then all his friends knew him again directly, and thought a great deal of him.

After a while he began to think it was very strange that no one could get a look at the princess. "Every one says she is very beautiful," he thought to himself; "but what is the use of that if she is to be shut up in a copper castle surrounded by so many towers. Can I by any means get to see her? Stop! where is my tinder-box?" Then he struck a light and in a moment the dog, with eyes as big as tea-cups, stood before him.

"It is midnight," said the soldier, "yet I should very much like to see the prin-cess, if only for one moment."

The dog disappeared instantly, and before the soldier could even look round, he returned with the princess. She was lying on the dog's back asleep, and looked so lovely, that every one who saw her would know that she was a real princess. The soldier could not help kissing her, true soldier as he was. Then the dog ran back with the princess; but in the morning, while at breakfast with the king and queen, she told them what a singular dream she had had during the night, of a dog and a soldier, that she had ridden on the dog's back, and had been kissed by the soldier.

"That is a very pretty story, indeed," said the queen. So the next night one of the old ladies of the court was set to watch by the princess's bed, to discover whether it really was a dream.

The soldier longed very much to see the princess once more, so he sent for the dog

again in the night to fetch her. But the
old lady put on water-boots, and ran after
him, and found that he carried the princess
into a large house. She thought it would

help her to remember the place if she made
a large cross on the door with a piece of
chalk. Then she went home to bed, and
the dog returned with the princess. But
when he saw that a cross had been made

on the door of the house where the soldier
lived, he took another piece of chalk and
made crosses on all the doors of the town.

Early the next morning the king and
queen accompanied the old lady and all the
officers of the household, to see where the
princess had been.

"Here it is," said the king, when they
came to the first door with a cross on it.

"And here is one, and there is another!"
they all exclaimed.

So they felt it would be useless to search
any farther. But the queen was a very
clever woman; she could do a great deal
more than merely ride in a carriage. She
took her large gold scissors, cut a piece of
silk into squares, and made a neat little
bag. This bag she filled with flour, and
tied it round the princess's neck; and then
she cut a small hole in the bag, so that the
flour might be scattered on the ground as
the princess went along. During the night
the dog came again and carried the princess on his back, and ran with her to the
soldier, who loved her very much.

The dog never noticed the flour as it fell

all along the road from the castle to the
soldier's room. The next morning the king
and queen saw clearly where their daughter
had been, and the soldier was immediately
arrested, and put in prison.

There he had to stop. It was dull and
gloomy enough, and all they said to him
was, "You will be hanged to-morrow!"
That was not exactly cheering, and his
tinder-box was left behind in his lodgings.
The next morning, through the bars of his
window, he saw a shoemaker's lad, in his
apron and slippers, who was running so
fast that one of his slippers fell off, and
flew right up against the window.

"Hallo! my lad," cried the soldier;
"just run to my lodgings, and fetch me
my tinder-box; you shall have a shilling
for your trouble."

The lad thought he should like to earn
the shilling, so he fetched the tinder-box,
gave it to the soldier, and——well, now
we shall hear.

The gallows was set up outside the
town, and round it stood the soldiers and
thousands of people. The king and queen

sat on a splendid throne, opposite the
judges and council. The soldier mounted
the ladder, the rope was placed round his
neck, when he begged permission to smoke
a pipe of tobacco.

The king granted his request, and the
soldier struck his box—once, twice, thrice!
In a moment, up sprang the three dogs.

"Help me, so that I shall not be
hanged!" said the soldier. And the dogs
flew at the judges and the council.

That frightened the people to such a
degree, that they cried out, "Noble soldier!
you shall be our king, and marry the
princess."

The Buckwheat.

VERY often, after a violent thunder-
storm, a field of buckwheat appears black-
ened and singed, as if a flame of fire had
passed over it. The country people say
that this appearance is caused by lightning;
but I will tell you what the sparrow says,
and the sparrows heard it from an old

willow-tree which grew near a field of buckwheat, and is there still. It is a large, venerable tree, though a little crippled by age. The trunk has been split, and out of the crevice grass and brambles grow. The tree bends forward slightly, and the branches hang quite down to the ground just like the green hair. Corn grows in all the surrounding fields, not only rye and barley, but oats—pretty oats that, when ripe, look like a number of little golden canary-birds sitting on a bough. The corn has a smiling look, and the heaviest and richest ears bend their heads low as if in pious humility. Once there was also a field of buckwheat, and this was exactly opposite to the old willow-tree. The buckwheat did not bend like the other grain, but erected its head proudly and stiffly on the stem. "I am as valuable as any other corn," said he, "and I am much handsomer; my flowers are as beautiful as the bloom of the apple blossom, and it is a pleasure to look at us. Do you know of anything prettier than we are, you old willow-tree?"

And the willow-tree nodded his head, as if he would say: "Indeed I do."

But the buckwheat spread itself out with pride, and said: "Stupid tree; he is so old that grass grows out of his body."

There arose a very terrible storm. All the field-flowers folded their leaves together, or bowed their little heads, while the storm passed over them, but the buckwheat stood erect in its pride.

"Bend your head as we do," said the flowers.

"I have no occasion to do so," replied the buckwheat.

"Bend your head as we do," cried the ears of corn; "the angel of the storm is coming; his wings spread from the sky above to the earth beneath. He will strike you down before you can cry for mercy."

"But I will not bend my head," said the buckwheat.

"Close your flowers and bend your leaves," said the old willow-tree. "Do not look at the lightning when the cloud bursts; even men cannot do that. In a flash of lightning, heaven opens, and we can look in; but the sight will strike even human beings blind. What then must happen to us, who only grow out of the earth, and are so inferior to them, if we venture to do so?"

"Inferior, indeed!" said the buckwheat. "Now I intend to have a peep into heaven." Proudly and boldly he looked up, while the lightning flashed across the sky as if the whole world were in flames.

When the dreadful storm had passed,
the flowers and the corn raised their droop-
ing heads in the pure still air, refreshed by
the rain, but the buckwheat lay like a weed
in the field, burnt to blackness by the lightning. The branches of the old willow-tree

rustled in the wind, and large water-drops
fell from his green leaves as if the old
willow were weeping. Then the sparrows
asked why he was weeping, when all around
seemed so cheerful, and he told them the
story of the buckwheat.